This Little Tiger book belongs to:

Lucy

Well done!

Love Miss Hutchinson

For Mark, James, Joe & Jess ~ J H

*For Julia, Angus, Mitch, Cathy, Clay and
all the Stone crew . . . my lovely, inspiring
Aussie friends, thank you ~ C P*

LITTLE TIGER PRESS
1 The Coda Centre, 189 Munster Road, London SW6 6AW
www.littletiger.co.uk

First published in Great Britain 2009
This edition published 2010

Text copyright © Julia Hubery 2009
Illustrations copyright © Caroline Pedler 2009
Julia Hubery and Caroline Pedler have asserted their rights
to be identified as the author and illustrator of this work
under the Copyright, Designs and Patents Act, 1988

Printed in China • LTP/1900/0883/0314

10 9 8 7 6 5 4 3 2

A Friend Like You

Julia Hubery   Caroline Pedler

LITTLE TIGER PRESS
London

Panda stretched happily in the morning sun. It was the first day of spring, time for his special journey up into the mountains.

Sunlight sparkled in the trees as Panda walked through the peaceful forest. Suddenly, a nut hit him on the nose. It was Monkey!

"Where are you going, Panda?" he giggled. "Anywhere fun?"

"Somewhere with a beautiful
secret," said Panda. "Do you want
to come too?"
  "Yes please!" squealed Monkey.
"I love secrets!"

As they set off, Monkey danced around Panda, hurrying him along. "Come on," he squeaked. "I want to see the secret!"

"Slow down, little friend," said Panda. "It's a long way. We have to cross Silver River first, then follow the rocky stream to the mountain meadows."

"That sounds easy," said Monkey. "Let's get going, Panda-plod!" and he raced ahead.

Panda padded on in the leafy
shade. As he stopped to chew
some bamboo, he heard a
chirrup under the leaves.
There he found a lovely bird,
bright as a jewel.

"Monkey, come and see this!" he called.
But Monkey was out of sight.
"Poor Monkey," thought Panda.
"In such a rush, he never sees anything!
I wonder where he's got to?"

Before long, Panda
found him chasing his
tail round a tree.
"You've been ages," said Monkey,
"and I couldn't find the silly river!"
"If you hush a minute, you'll hear
it," said Panda. "We're almost there."

"But I'm too excited to hush!" laughed Monkey, chattering away as they strolled on together.

Soon they reached
the banks of Silver River.
"I'm going to swing across,"
boasted Monkey. "Watch me fly, Panda!"
"Be careful!" Panda called out, as
Monkey leapt up into the branches.

Panda swam slowly down into the cool
water, smiling as a shoal of flickering
fish tickled by his toes.

Monkey came swinging
through the treetops.
   "I'll beat you across,
old soggy-ploddy-bear!"
he shouted.

"One,
two,
three,
whheeeeee,
look at
meeeeee!"

Monkey let go of his branch,
and soared up, up through
the glorious sky . . .

. . . then down,

Splash!

into the river.

"Help!" he shrieked.

"Here I am," shouted Panda. "Hold on tight!"
He pulled the squidgy, shivering monkey
from the water and swam to the shore.

"Poor little monkey-mess! However did
I find a friend like you?" Panda laughed.
"Come on – have a ride on my back!"
Monkey snuggled into Panda's cosy
fur. "Thank you, Panda," he whispered.

Up and up Panda climbed through
the misty foothills.

"Monkey, did you ever see anything
so pretty?" he gasped, but there was
no answer. Monkey was fast asleep.

"Sleep well, little friend," Panda
whispered, and padded softly on.

At last they reached the lush green meadows.
"Are we there?" squeaked Monkey,
bouncing awake. "Can I see the secret now?"
"It's up in the highest meadow," said Panda.
"The mountain butterflies are about to fly –
it's an amazing sight!"

"Quick, I want to see them!"
Monkey squealed.

"Wait!" called Panda. "I can't keep up."

"But they'll fly away!" Monkey cried,
skipping off. Panda sighed sadly and
climbed slowly after him.

When Panda reached the top, Monkey was looking very cross. "There aren't any butterflies!" he snapped. "We've missed them, all because you're such a slowcoach!"

"That's not very fair," cried Panda. "I can't rush like you. It's just the way I am."

Monkey hung his head. "I'm sorry, Panda," he said. "I know I'm lucky to have a friend like you."

Panda smiled. "Don't worry, little Monkey," he said gently. "All we have to do now is wait – ever so quiet, and ever so still."

Monkey snuggled next to Panda, and slowly, slowly, slowly . . .

. . . a thousand butterflies stretched their
wings, and flew into the air.

"They're amazing!" Monkey whispered.
"Thank you, Panda."

Panda hugged him and smiled. "I'm happy
I can share them with a friend like you."

Uplifting stories of friendship
from Little Tiger Press

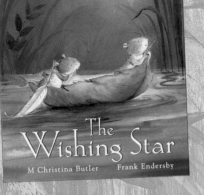

The
Wishing Star

M Christina Butler Frank Endersby

STEVE SMALLMAN

THE LAMB
WHO CAME FOR
DINNER

JOËLLE DREIDEMY

The
Little
Lost
Robin

Elizabeth Baguley
Tina Macnaughton

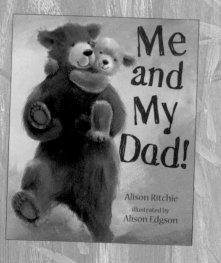

Me
and
My
Dad!

Alison Ritchie
illustrated by
Alison Edgson

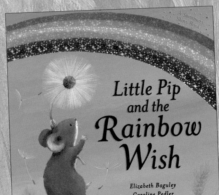

Little Pip
and the
Rainbow
Wish

Elizabeth Baguley
Caroline Pedler

Ted, Bo and Diz
The First Adventure

Jason Chapman

For information regarding any of the above
titles or for our catalogue, please contact us:
Little Tiger Press, 1 The Coda Centre,
189 Munster Road, London SW6 6AW
Tel: 020 7385 6333 • Fax: 020 7385 7333
E-mail: contact@littletiger.co.uk • www.littletiger.co.uk